Princess Truly

and

the Hungry Bunny Problem

by Kelly Greenawalt

I would like to thank Donald Grace, Chuck Greenawalt, Erin Williams, Heather Wrigley, Carole Henehan, Shannon McLean and Michele Morgan - without your patience, love and advice this book would not have come to fruition. I would also like to thank my sweet mother, Sherry Buckner for years of delightful and inspiring bedtime stories. An extra special thank you to Amariah Rauscher for making this dream come true. ~ Kelly

Princess Truly and The Hungry Bunny Problem
Text Copyright © 2012 Kelly Greenawalt
Illustrations Copyright © 2012 Amariah Rauscher

North Charleston, SC

ISBN-13: 978-1475288599
ISBN-10: 147528859X

Library of Congress Control Number: 2012920460

The text of this book is set in 15pt Minion Pro font.
The illustrations in this book were created using watercolor and charcoal.

Visit the author on the web! www.trulygirls.com
To purchase prints directly from the illustrator visit www.theextentofsilence.etsy.com.

For Kitty and Moo. Momma loves you. ~ K.G.

For Junie and JJ ~ A.R.

This is Princess Truly. She lives at the tippy top of a tall tower with her snuggly pug Sir Noodles. Princess Truly has curly black hair that is puffy like a cloud and full of magic. She also has a very loving heart.

She reads many books, asks many questions and is especially good at solving problems. People from all over the land come to ask the princess for help because she is such a clever girl.

One warm and sunny summer afternoon, Princess Truly and Sir Noodles were playing outside near the tower when the princess heard a very sad sigh.

"Did you make that sad sigh, Sir Noodles?" asked the little princess.

Sir Noodles shook his wrinkly head from side to side. It most certainly was not his sigh.

But where did it come from? Princess Truly decided to investigate and a very curious Sir Noodles decided to follow her. Just beyond the tower, they found a very sad Lola Little.

Lola was a gentle girl that loved animals, especially rabbits. In fact, some of her very best friends were bunnies. One bunny in particular followed her everywhere she went and his name was Bun. Bun's favorite past time was eating and his favorite person was Lola, mostly because she fed him lots of crunchy carrots but also because she always rubbed behind his long white ears.

"Good afternoon Lola, why are you so sad?" said the Princess.

"I planted carrots," said Lola sniffling "and they will not grow. If the carrots do not grow, I can not feed my very hungry bunnies."

"Oh goodness," said Princess Truly "that is very troubling news."

"Can you help me solve my hungry bunny problem?" asked Lola.

"I would be delighted to help," beamed the little princess "and so would Sir Noodles."

Sir Noodles raised his wrinkly eyebrow. He was very sleepy but he supposed he could help.

Bun was so excited his little nose twitchy-twitched and he hopped right over to Sir Noodles to thank him.

Sir Noodle's long slurpy tongue fell out of his slobbery mouth and he licked the little white rabbit. Instantly they were friends.

And so they set off. Princess Truly and Lola Little walked hand in hand. Bun hopped beside them and Sir Noodles waddled behind them. They crossed Crickety Creek.

Passed under the giant oak.

And looked both ways before crossing Dusty Road. Finally they arrived at Lola's garden.

Sir Noodles, who was exhausted from the long journey, found a shady spot under the apple tree where he could rest. Bun sat down beside him.

"This is my garden," said Lola "And here is where I planted the carrot seeds that will not grow."

"I see," said the princess, "There is not a single carrot."

"And my bunny is so hungry" said Lola.

hmmmm

"I once read a book that taught me about gardening" said Princess Truly. "I learned that in order for vegetables to grow they need lots of sunshine, plenty of water and fertile soil - which is a fancy name for good dirt."

"Plenty of water? Oh rats! I forgot to water the seeds!" said Lola Little.

"We may have found the problem then," said the Princess.

"But how will we solve it," wondered Lola.

"Do you have a bucket?" asked the princess.

Lola most certainly did. Princess Truly explained that they could use the bucket to fetch water down at Crickety Creek.

And so they set off...

They looked both ways when they crossed Dusty Road. They passed under the giant oak and carefully walked to the bank of Crickety Creek to fill Lola's bucket with water. When the bucket was full to the very top, they skipped back to the garden.

ah uh ah uh

Unfortunately they skipped so swiftly that they did not notice that the bucket was empty until they reached the garden.

"Oh rats!" cried Lola "The bucket is empty!"

"There appears to be a hole in the bucket. Unfortunately our solution has a problem of its own." said the princess.

"Yes," agreed Lola, who was starting to feel less hopeful and much sadder.

"Sniffly Sniff," added Bun, who was starting to feel much hungrier.

Now Princess Truly did her very best thinking when she snuggled her pug. So she sat down beside Sir Noodles. She rubbed his soft, velvety ears and kissed his wrinkly head.

"Thinkety Think," she said out loud which made Lola giggle.

"Peep! Thinkety! Peep!" said a little bird in the apple tree as she fluffed and fluttered nearly falling off the branch.

PEEP!

PEEP!

PEEP!

"Oh! Little blue bird, that is a fantastic idea! I need to fluff and flutter," said Princess Truly.

"I am very confused," said Lola Little.

"I suppose I do need to explain," said the princess.

"A long time ago, when I was just a baby princess, a ray of sunshine reached down from the sky and got caught in my curly hair. It swirled and twirled. It gleamed and it glowed. It sparkled and it shined," said the princess.

"And then?" said Lola.

"And then my curly hair was full of magic," said Princess Truly "Sometimes when I have a problem, my hair has an extra special solution."

"We sure need an extra special solution!" said Lola.

Princess Truly fluffed and shook her magical puffy hair. Her curls twisted and sparkled. They gleamed and they glowed. The wind began to swirl and twirl. It whipped and it whistled. It bustled and blustered and blew. Bun's little bunny nose twitched with excitement. And then the sunny sky was filled with the most peculiar purple clouds.

"Something truly magical is happening," said Lola.

"Truly!" said the little blue bird.

"Ow wow wooo!" barked Sir Noodles.

And just then, water began to fall from the peculiar purple clouds in the sky. Big fat rain drops plopped on the fertile soil. Little bitty rain drops danced all over the garden. This was no ordinary rain. It was full of magic. And soon the garden was full of little green sprouts. It rained and rained. The sprouts grew and grew. And before their eyes, giant crunchy carrots appeared.

"Oh wow!" said Lola.

"Peep!" said the little blue bird.

"What an extraordinary rain!" said Princess Truly.

"Now all the bunnies will have plenty to eat!" said Lola.

Bun shared some of his carrots with his friend, Sir Noodles.

crunch
crunch
munch

Sir Noodles made a funny face. He decided that pugs do not like carrots very much even though they are the same color as yummy cheese.

Princess Truly and her magical hair solved the hungry bunny problem. Now all the little bunnies in the land would have plenty to eat. Lola Little and all her bunny friends thanked the soggy princess and waved goodbye as their new friends set off for their tower.

The End

CPSIA information can be obtained
at www.ICGtesting.com
Printed in the USA
LVIC06n1039061213
364197LV00010B/81